Safari Animals™

HIPPOS

Amelie von Zumbusch

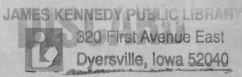

PowerKiDS press™

New York

Published in 2007 by The Rosen Publishing Group, Inc.
29 East 21st Street, New York, NY 10010

First Edition

Book Design: Erica Clendening

Photo Credits: Cover, pp. 1, 9, 11, 13, 17, 24 (bottom right) © Digital Vision; p. 5 © Digital Stock; pp. 7, 15, 21, 24 (top right, bottom left) © Artville; p. 19, 24 (top left) Boleslaw Kubica/www.istockphoto.com; p. 23 © Peter Johnson/Corbis.

Library of Congress Cataloging-in-Publication Data

Zumbusch, Amelie von.
  Hippos / Amelie von Zumbusch. — 1st ed.
     p. cm. — (Safari animals)
  Includes index.
  ISBN-13: 978-1-4042-3617-2 (library binding)
  ISBN-10: 1-4042-3617-1 (library binding)
  1. Hippopotamus—Juvenile literature. I. Title.
  QL737.U57Z86 2007
  599.63'5—dc22
                                    2006019456

Manufactured in the United States of America

CONTENTS

The hippo is a large animal. The word *hippo* is short for *hippopotamus*.

Hippos are very big. They can weigh as much as 7,000 pounds (3,175 kg).

Hippos have large mouths. Hippos can open their mouths 4 feet (1.2 m) wide.

Hippos live in rivers and lakes in Africa.

Hippos stay in the water most of the time. This keeps their skin from drying out.

13

A hippo's nostrils are on top of its mouth. This lets the hippo breathe when it is mostly underwater.

Hippos leave the water to eat. They eat grass. Hippos often eat at night.

Baby hippos are sometimes born underwater. A baby hippo is called a calf.

A group of hippos is called a herd. Herds of hippos rest together in the water.

Birds often sit on a hippo's back or head. They keep the hippo clean by eating bugs on its skin.

23

Words to Know

calf

herd

nostrils

skin

Index

Web Sites

Due to the changing nature of Internet links, PowerKids Press has developed an online list of Web sites related to this book. This site is updated regularly. Please use this link to access the list: www.powerkidslinks.com/safari/hippo/